Praise for *Astra the Lonely Airplane*

"Meet Astra, a private luxury jet who has a lot of big feelings to express! Children will identify with the emotional upheaval Astra experiences that comes from saying goodbye to a beloved friend and then, after an uncertain journey, moving to a new home. The illustrations are bright and accessible, and the rhyme scheme will delight young readers."

—Julie Bogart, author of *The Brave Learner*, creator and founder of the online writing and literature program Brave Writer

"*Astra the Lonely Airplane* is a sweetly told story of one little plane's journey to find new purpose and joy. The book progresses in rhyming couplets; something that is not only fun for children but also holds their attention and enhances their understanding of language. The bright illustrations invite children to empathize with the character's feelings of loneliness, uncertainty, friendship, and hope. Along the way, they will also learn some fun facts about airplanes and can imagine what it is like to travel across the country. The glossary and accompanying worksheets are a wonderful addition to this lovely and educational book. Until they can read Astra's next adventure, children will look forward to keeping her company by reading this one over and over!"

—Rev. Andrea Raynor, M.Div., United Methodist minister, hospice chaplain and spiritual counselor, and author of *The Voice that Calls You Home*, *A Light on the Corner,* and others

"It's rare that a children's book teaches such a broad range of lessons. *Astra the Lonely Airplane* educates young readers not only about planes and geography, but also about overcoming hardship and adversity, and embracing new circumstances that may occur in their lives. The fact that it's done in such a fun and entertaining way is a total home run for parents and kids."

—Rocky Boiman, former NFL linebacker, host on 700WLW in Cincinnati, college football analyst for ESPN, and author of *Rocky's Rules*

More praise for *Astra the Lonely Airplane*

"My third-grade class loved *Astra the Lonely Airplane*! The vocabulary sparked their interest in airplanes. Questions about the pilot, how planes are flown, and who flies in these types of planes were discussed. They are excited for the next book! As a teacher, I love seeing their enthusiasm about books. I can't wait to get a copy for the kids to read themselves."

—Amy Shuck, third-grade teacher

"*Astra the Lonely Airplane* is an easy-to-read rhyming book with a message—something I really appreciate as a mental health professional! This clever book helps children see how to navigate uncertain circumstances through the eyes of a whimsical jet airplane. You can feel the adventure of the story, complete with a fun happy ending."

—Tammy Wynn, LISW, MHA, RVT, owner of Angel's Paws, licensed pilot

"*Astra the Lonely Airplane* is a beautiful children's book that employs rhythmic sequencing and the use of personification to connect with the young reader. The illustrations are brilliant, and supplemental materials connect the young reader with the industry of air travel. In an age in which rapid changes to our society can create feelings of isolation, *Astra The Lonely Airplane* re-assures children that there is a place where all of us are valued and are able to make important contributions."

—Jeff Brokamp, senior vice president, junior achievement, retired administrator, Cincinnati Public Schools

ASTRA
the LONELY AIRPLANE

Story by
JULIE WHITNEY

Illustrations by
MICHELLE SIMPSON

BELLE ISLE BOOKS
www.belleislebooks.com

Copyright © 2022 by Julie Whitney

No part of this book may be reproduced in any form or by any electronic or mechanical means, or the facilitation thereof, including information storage and retrieval systems, without permission in writing from the publisher, except in the case of brief quotations published in articles and reviews. Any educational institution wishing to photocopy part or all of the work for classroom use, or individual researchers who would like to obtain permission to reprint the work for educational purposes, should contact the publisher.

ISBN: 978-1-953021-41-0
LCCN: 2021916479

Printed in the United States of America

Published by
Belle Isle Books (an imprint of Brandylane Publishers, Inc.)
5 S. 1st Street
Richmond, Virginia 23219

BELLE ISLE BOOKS
www.belleislebooks.com

belleislebooks.com | brandylanepublishers.com

To Captain Dan,
the finest pilot and husband in all the land;

And to my beautiful mom, Sandie,
who has always been my biggest fan;

And to those employed in the aviation industry
who lost their jobs in the pandemic of 2020

Astra was a lovely airplane—big, shiny, and white—
With black and red stripes down her left and her right.

At fifty-five feet long and standing twenty-two feet tall,
Astra could best be described as anything but small.

She had two big, powerful engines
and fifty-five-foot wings,
And flying superfast was
her very favorite thing.

At six hundred miles per hour,
she could climb to 45,000 feet.
Yes, Astra was indeed
one of the finest in the fleet.

Inside, she had a big, soft couch and comfy leather seats,
And a galley filled with soft drinks and yummy tasting treats.

She had a giant TV screen and a refrigerator, too.
In fact, you could say she was a mini house that flew!

She had a playful sense of humor and a smile for all she met—
Everything you could ask for in a big luxury jet.

The kind man who flew Astra was known as Captain Dan,
One of the finest pilots in (or over!) all the land.

He washed and waxed Astra, filled her tires with air,
Fueled her tank up weekly, and gave her lots of care.

Yes, Captain Dan and Astra made for a perfect team.

Their life was very magical—or so, that is, it seemed.

Until one day, Captain Dan came in without his usual smile.

"Astra, I'm afraid you'll be sitting in your hangar for a while."

He told his good friend Astra that she was being sold,
And any plans for flying would now be put on hold.

He said, "Keep your nose up, Astra, and try not to frown."
But Astra couldn't help but feel a little glum and down.

He promised to check in on her each and every week.
And with that, a big tear dropped down Astra's shiny cheek.

When Captain Dan left Astra, she felt very much alone.

And Astra wondered whether she would ever again be flown.

The days were long, and the nights were cold.

The snacks in her galley began to grow mold.

Astra needed to fly and get a bit of fresh air.

Being stuck inside her hangar was more than she could bear.

As the weeks turned into months, Astra couldn't help but cry,

Wondering if, when the time came, she would remember how to fly.

Her tires were flat, and her battery was low.

She sighed, "It doesn't matter; I have no place to go."

Until one day, a man arrived, hoping to buy her.

He looked Astra over and kicked at her flat tires.

He scowled and said, "Humph, this plane is too old,
And what is that strange smell—could it be mold?"

"But let's take her up and see what the old gal can do."
And so higher and higher clever Astra flew.

She chuckled as she flew him through a giant storm cloud.
"This will teach him for being so rude and loud!"

As Astra tossed and turned, the man started to feel ill.
He shouted, "Is there any way to make this plane hold still?"

He turned quite green as Astra made a very steep descent.
She could hardly wait to rid herself of this ill-mannered gent.

After Astra landed, the man crawled out on all fours,
And Captain Dan escorted him out the hangar doors.

Next, a man came by, who was quite large and tall,
And complained, "This plane may be a little too small."

He climbed aboard Astra, which was no easy feat—
His legs were so long he had to squeeze into his seat.

He struggled with his seat belt, which was far too short,
As Astra took off with a chuckle and a snort.

The man's head hit the ceiling and his arms hit the floor,
And he shouted, "I don't think I can take anymore!"
So Astra took a nose dive, and as she started to fall,
She laughed, "This will teach him, once and for all!"
"I certainly won't be buying this plane!" said the man,
And Astra grinned proudly at Captain Dan.

Next, in waltzed a well-dressed lady—perhaps a frequent flier?
Astra hoped and prayed that maybe this would be her buyer.

But as they flew, the lady said, "This plane is much too hot!
I think I would be happier just sailing on my yacht!"

So Astra cranked her air conditioning as high as it would go,
Then the lady put on her coat and gloves as the air began to blow.

"This plane's too cold," the lady said. So Astra cranked her heat,
And by the time they landed, the lady was red as a beet.

As the lady strutted off, complaining she was hot,
Astra began to worry that she never would be bought.

There had to be someone out there who would want to buy her,
Who wouldn't just laugh as they kicked at her tires,

Or complain that she was too old or too small,
Or too cold or too hot, or about anything at all.

Then Captain Dan said, "Here, let me fill up your tires.
You just need to be patient—we will find the right buyer."

"I'll wash and wax you till you're shining like new
And restock your galley with fresh, yummy treats, too."

And just as Captain Dan finished cleaning Astra up,
There finally came a great change in their luck.

For in strolled a man with a big, pleasant smile.

He looked Astra over, humming all the while.

"She's a beauty," he said, "so shiny and clean.

About the prettiest plane I think I've ever seen!"

He looked inside at her big, comfy seats
And checked out the galley with her fresh, tasty treats.

And then he proclaimed, "I think this plane is just right!
Can she make it all the way to California tonight?"

"Sure thing, I'll fill up her tank," said Captain Dan,
And he ran off to file a cross-country flight plan.

But first, he said to Astra, "We'll soon have a new home!
No more nights spent in your hangar alone!"

Astra was excited, but she was a little bit scared.
She'd never seen California—would she like it there?

But Captain Dan assured her, "We have nothing to fear;
It's beautiful, with rain just a few times a year."

So Astra took off and climbed higher and higher.
"This is such a smooth ride," marveled Astra's new buyer.

Once Astra reached a height of 45,000 feet,
The nice man relaxed and kicked up his feet.

"What a magnificent view—I really love this plane,"
He said as he looked down at the colorful terrain.

Across the Ohio and Mississippi Rivers they flew,
Then over the Rocky Mountains—what a spectacular view!

The Arizona desert was a beautiful sight,
While below them, the daytime faded to night.

They passed through a rainbow as Astra began her descent.

"What a very lucky sign!" exclaimed the nice gent.

As she landed smoothly in the Golden State,

Astra felt happy about her new fate.

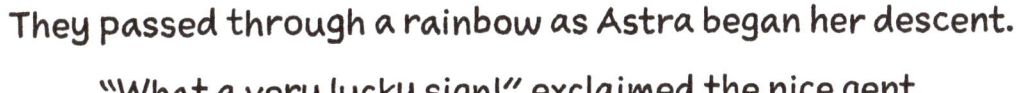

And although she was excited for what adventures lay ahead,
She was also quite jetlagged. It was almost time for bed!

So Captain Dan pulled her inside with the tug,
Then put his hands on her nose and gave her a hug.

As he covered her up and whispered, "Good night,"
Sweet Astra knew everything would be all right.

GLOSSARY OF PLANE TERMINOLOGY

Galley: The kitchen, which is located in the forward part of the cabin. It has drawers and cabinets full of food, two ice chests, a microwave, and even a coffee pot!

Lavatory: The bathroom, which is located at the rear part of the cabin. Just like a normal bathroom, it has a sink, toilet, mirror, and some storage cabinets.

Cockpit: This is where Captain Dan sits when he flies the plane. Everything on the plane can be controlled by knobs, switches, and levers in the cockpit.

Hangar: A large building with big sliding doors at one end—big enough for Astra and other planes to enter and park inside.

Altitude: The height above the ground or sea level.

Flight Plan: A detailed explanation of where a plane is going, how high and fast it will go, and who is on board. This is submitted by the pilot to air traffic controllers.

Tug: A tug, or tow tractor, is used to move large aircraft around an airport, flight line, and hangar.

Jetlag: Extreme tiredness felt after a long flight across several time zones.

SCAN HERE TO MEET THE _REAL_ ASTRA AND CAPTAIN DAN! ⟶

ABOUT ASTRA

Wingspan: The distance from the tip of one wing to the tip of the other. Astra's wingspan is fifty-four feet and seven inches, which is ten feet longer than a school bus!

Astra's Nose: There are many instruments inside Astra's nose which are used to communicate with air traffic controllers on the ground and let them know her position. There is also a radar, which shows Captain Dan any bad weather that lies ahead.

How Fast Can Astra Go? Astra's top speed is about 670 miles per hour, or Mach .875, which is 87.5% the speed of sound.

How High Can Astra Climb? Astra can fly as high as 45,000 feet above sea level.

What Is Her Cruising Altitude? On longer flights, Astra will usually cruise at 41,000 feet above sea level.

How Much Fuel Can Astra Hold? Astra can hold nearly 1,400 gallons of fuel.

How Often Do Her Engines Need to Be Run? The engines have to be run at least every twenty-eight days to keep them in top shape.

Emergency Equipment: Astra has life vests, oxygen masks, a first aid kit, and a life raft on board that may be used in the event of an inflight emergency.

About the Author

Julie Whitney is a public relations professional with forty years of experience in public relations and marketing, having worked on both the agency and client side as well as in the television industry. Her company, Phillippi-Whitney Communications, LLC, founded in 2000, represents both large and small clients in a wide variety of industries. She has promoted dozens of authors throughout her career, often supplementing the efforts of the internal PR teams of their publishers. She also works as on-camera talent, appearing in both television commercials and video podcasts. She even appeared as an extra in the movie *Grease*, which was shot on location in the summer of 1977 in Los Angeles.

Julie lives in Cincinnati with her husband Dan, a corporate pilot upon whom the character of Captain Dan is based. A naval aviator and USNA grad, he flew the P-3 Orion on active duty, and has flown a Gulfstream G100 (Astra) for the past thirteen years. With four grown children, they are now empty nesters and love spending time with their black Lab, Brody. They also enjoy traveling, boating, golfing, and all types of physical fitness.

About the Illustrator

Michelle Simpson is a full-time illustrator based out of the Niagara Region of Canada. She graduated with a BAA in illustration from Sheridan College. Michelle's main focus is on children's book illustrations and educational material for kids. She has worked with many large publishing houses and has also created concept artwork and final backgrounds for season two of the children's TV show *Ollie: The Boy Who Became What He Ate* and season one of *Tee and Mo*.

Printed in the USA
CPSIA information can be obtained
at www.ICGtesting.com
LVHW071211191023
761237LV00011B/8